# THE HERMETIC MARRIAGE

## A Study in the Philosophy of the Thrice Greatest Hermes

# by Manly P. Hall

**ISBN-10 | 0-89314-841-5**
**ISBN-13 | 978-0-89314-841-6**

Cover Art: *"The Hermetic Androgyne" from a German Manuscript*

---

*Published by*

**THE PHILOSOPHICAL RESEARCH SOCIETY**
3910 Los Feliz Boulevard
Los Angeles, CA 90027 USA

*Telephone* 323.663.2167
*Fax* 323.663.9443
*Website* www.prs.org
*E-mail* info@prs.org

*Printed in the United States of America*

# CONTENTS

"THE HERMETIC ANDROGYNE" *from a German manuscript*

# PART I

# THE ORIGIN OF HERMETIC PHILOSOPHY

Thoth Hermes, the ibis-headed, was the Egyptian god of wisdom, learning, literature, and science. He is accredited with being the first to reveal the art of writing to the present human race. According to the records available, he lived in Egypt as a contemporary of Moses. Some authorities even claim that Moses and Hermes were one and the same person. The Greek name Hermes is taken from an ancient root, herm, which means the active, positive, radiant principle of Nature, sometimes translated "vitality" and known to ancient Masonry as the cosmic fire, *CHiram*, and later as Hiram Abiff.

Hermes Trismegistus, often called *Mercurius Ter Maximus*, dominated the philosophical and literary thought of the ancient world. His very name became a synonym of wisdom—in fact, he was revered as the personification of philosophy and erudition. He was regarded as the first Qabbalist, the first physician, the first alchemist and the first historian. The actual life of this demigod and king of the ancient Double empire of the Nile is obscured by that twilight which hides the origin of all peoples. By reason of his great wisdom and magical powers, Thoth was listed among the gods, until today many believe that he never existed at all outside of mythology. But if action and reaction are equal, then something more substantial than a mere legend must be the foundation for the towering superstructure of the Hermetic arts.

During the early periods of human growth, when the intelligence of man was scarcely above that of the animal, all education was controlled by the priestcraft. The ancient priests were called the shepherds of men, for they guarded the flocks of primitive human beings as the shepherd does his sheep. Both science and philosophy were outgrowths of religion; in fact, all our present day wisdom came originally into the world from between the pillars of the sanctuaries. Hermes was to ancient philosophy what Jesus is to Christianity—its light, its inspiration and its impetus. The Egyptian initiates of the Temple of Isis claimed, therefore, that Hermes was actually the writer of all books on philosophical and religious subjects; that the supposed human authors were merely amanuenses, who wrote down upon parchment or vellum the thoughts which this god impressed upon their consciousness. In scriptural terms, they were the pens and he the ever ready writer.

During his lifetime, Hermes Trismegistus is supposed to have actually written forty-two books. Some, however, are probably the work of the ancient Egyptian priests, for in their glory these serpent-crowned hierophants represented the wisest group of philosophers that ever lived upon this planet. Clemens Alexandrinus states that these Hermetic books were divided into six parts, each dealing with a separate subject under such headings as astronomy (and its inseparable companion, astrology), medicine, geography, the hymns to the gods, and other titles. During the ages that have passed, Hermes has come to be acknowledged as the godfather of science, particularly its chemical and medical branches. Even after the Christian Era, numerous works dealing with religion and philosophical subjects were dedicated to him, and the general term "Hermetic art" has been applied to practically all the abstruse sciences of the ancient, mediaeval, and modern worlds.

The Divine Pymander (more commonly known as *The Shepherd of Men*) and the Smaragdine Tablet found in the Valley of Hebron are the most famous of the Hermetic fragments.* These two works are probably authentic and contain many keys to the universal science of life of which Hermes was a master. Nearly all Hermetic thought was an elaboration of the principle of analogy contained in the great Hermetic axiom, "That which is above is like unto that which is below, and that which is below is like unto that which is above."

At the present time, nearly all the so-called Hermetic writings are said to be lost—only a few isolated remnants remain of what once must have been a magnificent collection of philosophical, medical and religious wisdom.

During the Middle Ages one particular branch of Hermetic thought—alchemy—gradually came into prominence and for several hundred years dominated all other branches. Alchemy may be defined as the "chemistry of life." Alchemy was the androgynous parent of chemistry, which was separated from its sire by the speculations of Roger Bacon and Boyle. While chemistry as a science dealt only with minerals, medicines, and essences, alchemy struggled with the more profound elements of macrocosmic and microcosmic relationships. Alchemy undoubtedly originated in Egypt, for there the secret of transmuting base metals into gold and of prolonging the life of the physical body indefinitely was thoroughly understood by the priestcraft. Ancient records tell us that the Chaldean sages knew how to rebuild their bodies, many of them living to be over a thousand years old. Many of the processes by which this was accomplished were

---

*See "The Lost Keys of Freemasonry" by Manly P. Hall

7

concealed under the sacred Egyptian rituals, such as the *Book of Coming Forth by Day*, which E. A. Wallis Budge has called *The Book of the Dead*.

In the Middle Ages when religion, divorcing philosophy, was wed to blind faith, there was a renaissance of the alchemical and Hermetic arts. They were revived by that type of mind which demands reason, logic and philosophy as well as hymns and prayers. Alchemy won numerous converts in Germany, France, and England. The long ignored works of the Arabian magicians enjoyed a wide popularity and from them was extracted the greater part of modern astrology. The ancient philosophies of the Jewish patriarchs were also revived and Qabbalism became a universal topic of consideration.

Paracelsus, the great Swiss physician (sometimes called the *second* Hermes), undoubtedly rediscovered the ancient Egyptian formulae of the *Philosopher's Stone* and the *Elixir of Life*, and around him rallied a coterie of mediaeval philosophers who stand out strongly against the dun-colored background of mediaeval culture. Back of this revival of interest in ancient Egyptian philosophy, we find the master minds and guiding hands of three great philosophical movements: (1) THE ORDER OF THE ILLUMINATI—represented by Mohammed, prophet of Islam; Roger Bacon, father of chemistry: and Paracelsus, father of modern medicine. It is an interesting fact that the present buildings and school of Rudolph Steiner, the German mystic, are located in the grounds of the old estate of Hohenheim where Paracelsus lived. (2) THE ORDER OF FREEMASONS—represented by the great Robert Fludd, master of symbolism and alchemy and Elias Ashmole, the philosopher unique. (3) THE ROSICRUCIANS—a sacred organization founded by the mysterious Father C.R.C. after his return from Arabia. In the mythological city of Damcar he had been educated in alchemy and astrology by

Arabian adepts. After him came Sir Francis Bacon, the remodeler of British law; Count Cagliostro, the sublime adventurer; and last and greatest of all, the great Comte de St. Germain, probably the world's greatest political reformer—an alchemist by fire. These superlative minds leavened the loaf of materiality and kept alight the flame of Hermes during the mediaeval centuries of religious intolerance and bigotry.

Concealed beneath chemistry—the science of relating chemicals and elements—these minds discovered the ancient Egyptian arcana, long hidden by the crafty priests of Ra and Ammon. Alchemy thereupon became the chemistry of the soul, for under the material symbol of chemistry was concealed the mystery of "The Coming Forth by Day." These ancient wise men taught that the world was a great laboratory; that living essences were the chemicals; that the span of life was a period of time given to the mind in which to experiment with the great agencies of Nature; and that to the thoughtful came wisdom from their labors, while for the thoughtless life held only foolishness and sorrow. In this great laboratory man learned how to combine the living chemicals of thought, action, and desire and by learning the ways of Nature became master of Nature. He became a God by actually becoming a man. In the words of the great Paracelsus, "the beginning of wisdom is the beginning of supernatural power."

Of all the Hermetic mysteries none is more perplexing than the so-called Hermetic marriage. A post-Christian interpretation of an ancient Egyptian ritual supposedly written two hundred years earlier was published to the modern world in the first part of the seventeenth century under the name of *The Chymical Nuptials of Christian Rosencreutz*. Little, if anything, has been discovered concerning the origin either of this book or the *Fama Fraternitatis* which appeared about the same time. The exalted

Order of Rosicrucian philosophers has been very reticent concerning its members and their works, and even today it is difficult to prove from a strictly material viewpoint that the Order ever existed. But concealed under the quaint wording of the alchemical marriage can be plainly traced a series of mysterious formulae concerning the transmutation of base metals into gold. The alchemist taught that man contained within himself all the elements of nature, both human and divine, and that by a special culture the base elements of his nature could be transmuted into the spiritual gold called the soul. In discussing this, Paracelsus makes plain that these philosophers did not wish to leave the impression that something could be made from nothing, but rather they emphasized the fact that each individual thing contains all other things and that the alchemical process of making gold was merely to culture the germ of gold which is contained in every base substance. Modern science substantiates the alchemical point of view by stating that it expects to extract gold from mercury by taking out or isolating the electron of gold, which is one of the constituents of every mercurial atom. Taking the chemistry of human relationships as a basis, therefore, we have prepared the following thesis concerning the true preparation of a Philosopher's Stone and the Elixir of Life according to the fundamentals laid down by Hermes and the ancient Egyptian priestcraft.

# PART II

# HERMETIC ANATOMY

A theory of natural creation has been generally accepted by the faiths of the world, with the possible exception of the Christian. To the ancients, everything in Nature was alive; therefore, they accepted the human body as symbolic of the universe. The Hebrews called this prototype *Adam Kadmon,* or the Grand Man, in whose mold all things were made. Every system of cosmogony, except the Christian, makes the universe a living thing. Instead of a God separated from his creation, the Brahmins, Jews, Persians and Chinese have conceived their God as being hopelessly involved in His creation. They have accepted more literally than the Christians the idea that man dwells in God— that in God he actually lives, moves and has his being. They call this God Macroprosopus, or "the spirit of the Grand Man." From his body was made the Macrocosm, consisting of suns, moons, planets, meteors, ethers, gases, and the sundry parts of creation. In the Scandinavian Eddas, the universe was formed from the body of Ymir, the frost king. In India the universe was constructed from the person of Brahma, whose members became the various bodies of the visible cosmos. The Hermetists, therefore, said "Man, know thyself! for thou, like God, are all wisdom and all power, and the shadow bearing witness unto the Eternal."

An anonymous alchemist, writing in the Middle Ages, stated; "God has given man three ways whereby he may learn the Infinite will: (1) NATURE, for in the stars that twinkle in the sky, the planets in their thundering march, and the earth with its multitude of laws, are concealed the laws of God; (2) HOLY WRIT, the inspired word of saints and sages unnumbered; and (3) ANATOMY, the structure of our own bodies, wherein is concealed the structure of the universe, for all things are made by one mold." The electron, revolving around its nebular center, obeys the same law that moves planets around the sun. In this we see the truth of the great Hermetic axiom, "as above, so below." As with the lesser, so with the greater.

The Hermetists spent much time studying the intricate construction of man and, like the Brahmans of India, they divided him into three major parts. In India this trinity of basic parts is called Adi, Buddhi, and Manas, meaning literally spirit, soul, and body. Their trimurti corresponds to the trinity of Christian theology. Each of these three major parts of a god, a man, or a universe was personified as an individual. *Adi* (spirit) was called the divine cause, or the Father. *Manas* (matter) was called the divine effect, being known in India as Shiva and in Christendom as the Holy Spirit. Between these two stood *Buddhi*—the mediator, the god-man, the Mercury of the Latins, the messenger of the gods. By some this intermediary is considered synonymous with soul; by others it is called mind, because man is the uniting link between life in the sense of energy and death in the sense of inertia. To the pagans and Hermetists, everything in Nature is alive—the ethers, the air, minerals, even the earth itself were endowed by the ancients with intelligence, consciousness, and feeling. The A*di-Buddhi-Manas* constitution of man is represented by he alchemists under the symbolism of the Philosopher's Stone and its three important constituents, salt, sulphur, and mercury. According to alchemy, salt is the substance of all things; it is the body, the form, the dense crystallized particles from which al physical things are manufactured. Sulphur is symbolic of fire, the divine agent. Fire is defined by the Hermetists as the life of all things, and is the Adi of the Brahman trimurti. Mercury, the universal solvent, becomes synonymous with Buddhi, the mind—the thing which absorbs all experience into itself—the link between God and Nature. All of the great World Saviors have come, it seems, as personifications of Buddhi, or the Universal Mediator. Like the Indian Vishnu, they have sought to bring God and man closer together. Whether as Christ, Prometheus, Zoroaster, Krishna, or Buddha, they have come to bear witness to the Father; and being made in the semblance of man, but imbued with the spirit of God, they have become personifications of the Universal Solvent.

To the Hermetists, man has always been considered androgynous, and they created the god Hermaphroditus to represent the duality of all living things. This word is coined from Hermes, fire or vitality, and Aphrodite, the goddess of water. The great Hermetic and alchemical adage was, "Make the fire to burn in the water, and the water to feed the fire. In this lies a great wisdom."

The ancient Rosicrucians taught that the eternal feminine was not extracted from the nature of man, as Moses would have us think, but was rather made subservient to the opposite side of its own nature. They believed that every creature was essentially male and female, but for reasons which we will discuss later, only one phase of that nature manifested at a time. By fire these philosophers taught that there was but one life force in the human body and that man used it in the furtherance of all his labors; that he digested his food with essentially the same energy with which he thought and reproduced his species with the same forces which he used in physical exercise. This force personified was said to be the builder of the Universal Temple. It became Hiram Abiff of Masonry, the builder of the Eternal Temple.

In Egypt, this force is symbolized by a serpent, and it is worthy of note that in the ancient Hebrew the words serpent and savior are synonymous. In The Stanzas of Dzyan an ancient Tibetan fragment, it is stated that at one time a shower of serpents fell upon the earth. This is understood, esoterically, to represent the coming of the great World Teachers, who have long been called "serpents." The Savior of the Aztecs and Incas was called Quetzalcoatl. This name means "feathered serpent." From the serpent kings of Egypt to the feathered serpents of Tibet, the serpent is symbolic of the vital energies of the human body. Moses raised the brazen serpent in the wilderness, and all who gazed upon it lived. Christ, the serpent reborn, says: "I, if I be lifted up, will draw all men unto me." The simile is obvious, yet few ever understand it. To the ancients, the magic wand was the spinal canal. Through this canal runs a sacred liquid, called "fire oil," in Greek Christos, the savior or redeemer of things. This same thought has been preserved for Masonry under the heading, "The Marrow of the Bone."

The Hermetic philosophers recognized this essence in man as a distillation of Universal Life derived from the atmosphere, the sunlight, the rays of the stars and food. This universal vitality, upon which all living things draw, is probably the origin of the myths of the gods who died for mankind. It is undoubtedly the origin of the legend of the Last Supper, for man eternally maintains himself upon the body and the blood of this spirit of universal energy.

If this energy (which passes through the conduit of the spine) is drained off by various parts of the body, it stands to reason that waste will ultimately result in want. We know that it is very undesirable to do heavy thinking directly after eating for at such times the vital energies are digesting food and cannot safely be diverted to other channels. By analogy, one-pointedness is the basis of success; for when the bodily energies are divided against each other, they cannot perform their proper functions. The ancients taught that the normal individual had two distinct avenues of expression —the first, mental and spiritual; the second, emotional and physical. The mental faculties were radiant, powerful, dominating, and strong, but often cruel and cynical. The mind was called the positive pole of the soul, while the heart was called the negative pole.

We have been taught that the spirit expresses itself through the mind; the soul and the body through the heart. The ancient alchemists called the mind "the sun" and the heart "the moon," for to them strength, reason and logic were masculine, paternal, solar powers; while love, beauty, intuition and kindliness were feminine, maternal, lunar qualities. This will probably make clear why gold and silver had to be blended in the great alchemical enterprises, for the gold and silver of the alchemists were not dead metals but living qualities in human life.

The marriage of the sun and moon was, therefore, the marriage of the heart and mind or the two halves of every nature. It was the union of strength with beauty, courage with inspiration; and in its greater sense, the union of science with theology, or God with Nature. The urgency of this alliance is evident in the world today, where cold intellectualism and commercialism need the finer sentiments of friendliness and altruism to offset their heartlessness.

On the other hand, fanaticism, blind faith and ungoverned emotionalism require the strong hand of logic and reason to steer them away from the rocks of insanity and death. Perfect equilibrium in the nature of people is seldom met with; in fact, it is Nature's greatest rarity. A person with that perfectly balanced viewpoint, however, is the living Philosopher's Stone, for he has strength matched with kindliness and justice tempered with mercy.

Hermetic anatomy teaches that there are two small bodies in the brain which are identified with the living Yin and Yang of China. In the same way, every person has a masculine nature and a feminine nature, and never do we find these two entirely dissociated. It may be that East Indian philosophy gives us our best light in this rather perplexing subject, for both the Hindus and the alchemists agree that the spirit is androgynous—as god, it is both father and mother. It states in Genesis, "God created man in His own image, male and female created He them." We could infer from this that God is both male and female, and as the spirit of man is of God, it must partake of the androgynous nature of its parent. In harmony with the Eastern sages, sex exists no more in spirit than it does in the embryo before the third month of prenatal life. Sex is a polarization of the body, a manifestation of spirit; but the germ of life itself is capable of projecting both the positive and negative rays.

We now become involved in a still more perplexing problem, namely, what governs the sex which the human is to manifest during life? Again we turn to the Eastern Sages. Evolution is the continuity of form appearing in cycles and gradually unfolding from a simple cell to a complex organism. If a form evolves, it is not absurd to suppose that the cause of that form is also evolving.

The Oriental solves one of the Western world's greatest problems by the law of reincarnation. This little-known doctrine (which was removed from the Christian faith, A. D. 550, at the Council of Constantinople) taught that the spirit or life is immortal; that it descends into gross matter not once but many times in order that it may ultimately gain that perfection which no living creature has ever yet gained in one appearance in the world. This doctrine also taught that the consciousness thus descending into form does not always appear in one sex, but alternates, first appearing in a masculine body and then in a feminine —in this way developing both sides of the nature symmetrically. If this doctrine be accepted, it will go far toward solving a number of problems concerning heredity and the so-called injustice and inequality in the world. Even without it, Hermeticism can still stand; with its aid, however, the alchemical philosophies become far more clarified.

The ancient wisdom teaches that the circle of the creative forces in the human body is broken at the present time. One end of this broken ring is in the brain, where it furnishes the power or vitality which is the basis of brain function. The other end of this circle is located in the generative system, where it furnishes the means of reproducing the species. At a time remote in history, man was a complete creative unit in himself, however, being capable of procreating his species like certain of the lower orders of animals of today. At that time, however, he had no mind. According to mythology, the raising of the brazen serpent therefore gave him a mind but broke the creative circuit. In the masculine sex the positive pole of the life force is in the brain; the negative pole is used for generative purposes. In the feminine sex, the negative pole is in the brain; the positive pole in used for generative purposes. As a direct outgrowth of this condition (temporarily maintained in order that man may think and develop his higher nature and at the same time offer opportunity for other lives to come into manifestation), the institution of marriage was established.

Marriage is, therefore, the Hermetic symbol of the ultimate reunion of the two halves of each individual's androgynous nature when, after repeated appearances and associations, equilibrium between these masculine and feminine qualities is established. The wedding ring was accordingly symbolic of the golden ring of the spirit fire, which connected the spiritual and material natures of every individual.

Ultimately the present methods of reproduction will be abolished and both halves of the spirit fire again turned into the brain. One of them now finds its polarity in the pituitary body and the other in the pineal gland. These two tiny ductless bodies, while an enigma to modern science, were recognized by the ancients as organs of great significance. The Ancient Wisdom teaches that the pineal gland was the original organ of vision, namely, the third eye, called in the Sanskrit Dangma, or the Eye of Shiva.

It is the all-seeing eye of the Masons, and the meaning of the word Buddha. In uniting its spark with the pituitary body, this gland fuses the broken circle, and thus consummates the Hermetic marriage, whereby through an immaculate conception in the brain the great light—the Shining One—is born as a luminous spark in the third ventricle, which is the Master Mason's chamber in the ancient and accepted rite.

Today students of the ancient wisdom are seeking to prepare themselves for this peculiar work. The Hermetic marriage is, therefore, an individual matter involving the attainment of individual completeness, requiring of the aspirant a sincere effort to be balanced, sane, and consistent in everything he does. In the alchemical retorts and vials we recognize the bodies, glands and organs of man; and in the chemicals, the essences and forces coursing through the body. With these the individual consciousness must labor until it is capable of combining them according to the perfect formula.

# PART III

# HERMETIC PHILOSOPHY IN FAIRY STORY

What child does not grow up in a fairyland extending from the first glimmer of understanding to the time when the grim realities of maturity tear down the dream world and replace it with hopelessness and despair? Hearts are broken all the way through this tragic pageantry of existence, but the first heartbreak is when the fairy stories and their wonderful little people are given up, and those beautiful beings with which we have peopled the world of our fancies give way to heartless human creatures of real existence.

Man thoughtlessly destroys not only the dreams of others, but makes his own world a nightmare peopled with hobgoblins of selfishness and egotism. The fairies of childhood are always benevolent, kindly, helpful, serving the poor in distress, righting wrongs, and doing many beautiful things; while the realities of later life are generally malevolent and productive of all the miseries that the fairies of childhood sought to heal with silver-tipped wand and rainbow dreams.

In the great game of life why can we not still preserve some of the beauty and romance of fairyland? The world of pixies, gnomes, and fairy godmothers is just as real in childhood as the grinding commercial system is during later life. Economics would suffer no injury nor would standards collapse if dreams were perpetuated and man instructed how to build solid foundations under his castles of ether, for human beings are ever children at heart. Man grows old but he never grows up; like Peter Pan, he is childlike from the cradle to the grave. Life for the average person has an insufficiency of beauty or sweetness with which to combat the sordid grind of modern things. Here and there one lives a whole life in a fairyland of poetry, art, or music. Such a one we call a dreamer. But as the years weigh heavy upon us, we forget Prince Charming and Princess Beautiful and ourselves become cruel old ogres who live to frighten other children's souls out of their dreams. Are not most of us in our daily lives akin to the same old cruel giants who dwelt alone in castles of gloom and over whom we shivered in terror and sorrow when we read fairy stories of long ago?

Will any child ever forget Cinderella and her wonderful glass slipper—how she met and won the beautiful prince while her envious sisters and cruel stepmother gnashed their teeth in rage? The story is part of childhood. But with the coming of years, poor little Cinderella is forgotten; the rag dolls are thrown in the corner; the toy blocks are covered with dust, for the dream world of childhood has faded from the mind, and little pattering feet once running hither and thither have given place to slow uncertain steps. Yet the romance finds another setting. Prince Charming becomes a soda-fountain clerk or floor-walker in a downtown store, while Princess Beautiful sells ribbons in some little country shop.

The lives of people are really fairy stories, in which they play out the comedies and tragedies of their lives, seeking for something today to take the place of shattered dreams of yesterday. Few of us have ever realized that fairy stories have their counterpart in Nature. The world about us is filled with ugly step-mothers and half-sisters who cannot wear glass slippers. They are not living people, it is true, but they are attitudes and thoughts; for our own dispositions, when perverted and soured, become hateful ogres and witches seeking to destroy goodness and kindness within ourselves.

Do you remember Beauty and the Beast—how, in spite of the sorcery that had turned the handsome prince into a hideous monster, the coming of Beauty into his life restored him again to human form and happiness? Through the lack of beauty in his own heart, many an individual has become a horrible, hideous beast, who while still in human shape has all the attributes of a ferocious animal.

How often the sense of beauty is the thing which redeems! Beauty of soul and beauty of life bring back happiness to the beast. We see it on the battlefield of Flanders, where flowers are springing up in the shadows of the trenches. In Nature we ever see Beauty redeeming the Beast. Out in the forest the dark, dead tree is gaunt and bare; but Nature with her magic wand covers the tree with creeping vines, decking its gaunt limbs with mantles of flowers and urging the birds to build their nests amid its dark branches. A beautiful word, a beautiful thought, a beautiful life—all these are magic wands which recall Prince Charming from the darkness of gloom and despondency.

Have you read the story of Sleeping Beauty? If not, go straight to the library and visit the children's room. Sit down on one of those little chairs about ten inches from the floor, get out the book with its colored pictures and much-thumbed pages, and go with the Prince through the great forest of nettles and thorns which surrounds the palace of Princess Beautiful. The Princess is under a spell which causes her to sleep until she is awakened by the handsome Prince, who passes through all the obstacles of life in order to claim her as his own.

Have you ever realized that you are both the Prince and Princess in one—that the Princess is your own better nature, the spirit of beauty lying asleep in you, hidden away behind walls of nettles and thorns of conflict? These thorns and briars are the struggles and disappointments and impediments of life, for there is a crown of thorns in every life. Man longs for the beautiful and the true, but he must always claim it from a heart of sorrow and sadness. Peace will never be found without labor, so go with the faith of a true prince into the world, which is the forest of nettles, for the world is filled with aggravating, pricking, tearing and wounding things. But if you will go through life with the faith of the fairy Prince, you will find that the thorns give way before you, that the nettles and briars part and let you through; for there is a reward for those who seek to beautify life and awaken the spirit of harmony lying asleep behind the briars of privation.

There is beauty in all things. If your life has been deprived of it, go forth like the Prince and claim it. Remember, however, that happiness must always be reached through the forest of thorns and that every spirit must be a hero to attain it.

Let us stop for a moment in passing and read over again those wonderful legends, The Thousand and One Nights—how Sinbad sailed the seven seas, and Ali Baba watched from his tree while the thieves hid their treasure in the mountain side. Fantastic stories these, but in every one a lesson. Every one is true, if we can but read the meaning aright.

Will you ever forget Aladdin and his wonderful lamp—how the poor beggar boy who lived with his widowed mother (Masons take note) won, by means of his magic lamp, everything in the world that his heart desired? He married the Princess Beautiful, overpowered the evil magician, and became Caliph of Bagdad. Here again life is unfolded to us. What is the lamp of Aladdin that gives him everything that he desires? The lamp is wisdom, which is gained under the ground in the darkness of the earth—meaning life and its complexities. The genii that serves it is Nature, who obeys all who understand her laws. The Princess is happiness, peace, and the spirit of eternal romance, which lead man in his quest and strengthen him that he may win the great battle of life; for in saving his own soul he wins the Princess of his dreams.

The evil magician is selfishness and his own lower nature which seek to prevent Aladdin from having the lamp, for the animal must die when man becomes human. Aladdin becomes the Caliph of Bagdad, which represents the attainment of God-hood or wisdom and the mastery of his own universe as a result of his exploits. All these stories have a meaning the child never suspects, but so deep that the sage cannot comprehend it all.

The greatest minds that ever lived have believed in fairies—if not embodied ones, at least in the principle of fairies. Socrates had his familiar spirit that comforted him in time of sorrow. Napoleon had his little red gnome, which was seen sitting on his shoulder at the battle of the Pyramids. Paracelsus declared that the fairies were elemental creatures and that the reason small children see them is because in early childhood the soft spot on the crown of the head has not completely closed and the pineal gland, or etheric eye, is still somewhat active.

# PART IV

# THE LOVE STORIES OF THE GODS

Romance fills the mythologies of every nation. They are the romances of natural forces, for in all the faiths of the world the creative powers of Nature are personalized. Human feelings and emotions are attributed to them. Idylls of beauty and pathos fill the scriptures of all peoples, and the sanctity of the highest forms of human sentiment is lauded as virtue by every spiritual message the world has ever received.

The ancients (speaking in the language of men) taught that the gods were the planets, and that the rays from these distant planets came as suitors bringing gifts to the earth. They taught that all things in Nature plighted their troth one to the other; that from these romances came forth the gods of creation and the spirits that labor with the universe in its forming.

In India, *Brahman*—the Father God, the life of all things—awakened the universal substance, *Matripadma*—the great Mother Lotus—by a ray of light which he caused to descend from the heavens. This ray of light, striking the Lotus, kissed it with a gleam of energy that vibrated through the entire blossom. Thereupon the blossom opened its petals and dropped its seeds which, falling into Chaos, were the beginnings of the worlds.

In the Greek legend of Orpheus and Eurydice we are told how the god of music and harmony wooed the goddess of beauty and love. Later because of the sting of the serpent Eurydice died and descended into the world of Pluto. Orpheus followed her into the depths of hell, seeking to win her back from the realm of death. Losing her at last, he wandered brokenhearted and alone to an untimely grave.

This myth (like the others) deals with the beauty of attitudes and is entirely impersonal, for Orpheus represents skill and Eurydice signifies inspiration. When she had been taken from his life, he could no longer play the harmonies which before had filled his soul. We often fail in life because of the lack of inspiration which adds soul to the dexterity of the fingers. Every life must not only have the power to accomplish: it must also have the inspiration to lead it on.

Here we have the laws of polarity at work in life. These are the two opposites—skill and inspiration. How easily one can destroy the other, yet how perfectly each complements the other! All things in Nature are at their summum bonum when each quality complements every other. Reason, logic, philosophy, courage, daring—even aspiration—are the masculine qualities. They lend strength to accomplishment, but they are incomplete unless there is added to them inspiration, intuition, grace, beauty, faith, and love—either love of labor or of the spirit behind labor.

From India comes what is probably the most beautiful of all love stories—the legend of Radha and Krishna. Out in the forest these two loved and played, and their romance has become one of the great spiritual inspirations of India.

Krishna was the spirit, gallant, beautiful, and dynamic—the Prince Charming of every love story—while Radha was the body, Nature, the eternal receptive thing. As the sun radiates its light upon the earth, so Krishna brought his gifts to the one he loved. In their story is played in the drama of the love of Life for Substance, and the romance in which Life redeems Substance through eternal devotion is a beautiful thing indeed. Krishna attained divinity, and through love, Radha—the soul—was liberated from the shell of substance and became one with the spirit of Light.

The analogy is ever-present in religion and Nature. From the bubbles of ether to the cells of the body, we find the universal law of polarity. We find the romance of electrons, the love story of the fire mist, the swirling ethers, the endless waves of the sea as they kiss the shore all manifesting divine romance. There is a sanctity, a divinity, in the lessons of Nature which makes us all better for the realization of our individual part in the joyous Plan.

Not God but man takes the romance out of life. By his selfishness, cruelty, licentiousness, and greed, man tears down the altar of Vesta and fills the world with degeneracy.

If the people would live the occult life, they would come to realize the beauty of comradeship and brotherly love, which are the keystone of the Universal Plan.

In the last analysis, we are all of one family, and not such a large family at that. We are living together on a little globe which is but a speck of dust in Chaos. With all our presumed mental growth, with all our philosophy and logic, we have not yet learned how to live at peace with one another. We have not yet learned the first principles of social relationships in the universe.

We have come to look upon contention as necessary. We have instituted a reign of hate to take the place of fraternity and kindliness, and time after time we have drenched the earth with the blood of our fellow creatures. We have loosed the beast that goes howling for destruction, slaying our fellow creatures for meat and trimming our clothing with the fur and feather of defenseless creatures whom we have slaughtered for our selfish ends. This was not the plan of Nature.

God made a garden and gave it to man. Man, having made of this garden a hell, now offers it back to God. But in the due course of things the wrong shall be made right, the errors shall pass away, and only the reality shall endure. Let each hasten that day by going (as did the Prince in the fairy story) to rescue Beauty from her long sleep. Let each awaken inspiration from the tomb wherein she has lain so long, thus adding to the material attributes of reason, logic, and law the spiritual attributes of grace, beauty, and ideality.

The world lives not by bread alone, but by hope. Each day man rises to his daily struggle fed by the spirit of hope. Even the most material of us dwells largely in the spirit of our dreams. That which builds and constructs in our dreams is Good; that which destroys is evil. For ages the spirit has been imprisoned by limitation, and this spark of hope within is the only light that has shone through the barred windows of the soul.

Did you ever think of the romance there is between the spirit and its hope, between the heart and the hand? Did you ever think that there is a marriage within man himself where his reason weds his dream; that his mind—masculine and domineering—is united in spiritual wedlock to the heart—kindly, sympathetic, and compassionate? This is the real romance of the gods. None shall ever reach wisdom until within himself these nuptials have been consummated and love and logic, hand in hand, guide the spirit in its search for understanding. Thus man is guided in his search for truth and led to the greater goal of cosmic understanding.

Neither matriarchy nor patriarchy alone can ever rule the world well, but when these two join forces, then the affairs of the world will be run as wisely as those of the gods. Then the Lords of Compassion will join with the Lords of Reason in molding the destiny of the universe.

# PART V

# NATURE, THE DIVINE INSTRUCTOR

Age after age man is forced to admit that Nature, an apparently unintelligent entity, is the final criterion of all his virtues and his vices. In order to survive, all things must be natural. Nature is eternally consistent. All things that are unnatural are false; all things that are natural are true. True does not mean good or bad, according to modern standards; it means harmony and consistency. It is natural to be consistent; it is unnatural to be inconsistent. To be consistent is to be happy; to be inconsistent is to be unhappy.

All visible things bear witness to that invisible spark of immortality which we call spirit. This spark is eternally unfolding; it is ever in the state of becoming. Man is a magnificent atom; the universe is a magnificent man. Every moment of life is a transition period—the passing out of an old into a new mental, spiritual or physical environment. The personality of the bodies ever bears witness to the changes taking place within the invisible spiritual atom. Birth, growth, and decay bear witness to the scope of function attained by the spiritual germ, which is the real "I" of every living thing. This "I" is ever molding bodies in the likeness of itself. Like the shadow, the body moves in consistency with its spiritual urge. Between them is perfect harmony. The body must bear witness, therefore, not only of the virtues of the consciousness but also of its ignorance and perversion.

As previously stated, harmony and happiness are correlated. Physical harmony is health, mental harmony is balance, and spiritual harmony is peace. Harmony is natural; inharmony is unnatural. To be unnatural is to be unhappy—in spirit, mind, or body, as the case may be. We live in an unnatural age, for nearly everything we do is inconsistent and unnatural. The food we eat is unnatural; the clothes we wear are unnatural; the thoughts we think are either artificial or morbid, or at least distorted by our own unnatural viewpoints concerning life. As a result, we are unhappy, sick, and rendered incapable of filling our proper places in the Great Plan. The white race has a preponderance of nervous wrecks who demand a civilization ever more complex to furnish thrills for their satiated nerves. The day of simple things is passing, and with it many of the finer sentiments of life. We do not mean that our day is devoid of advantages or our ethics of their redeeming features, but we do believe our culture to be assumed, our respectability largely a sham, and our virtue a veneer. Our entire code of life is unnatural, and consequently is doomed to destruction. It will carry down with it into dissolution those who have become dependent upon its fallacies.

As surely as physical disease is the result of an unnatural physical condition, so a diseased mentality is the outgrowth of unnatural mental activities. An unnatural emotional nature is a diseased one. And, what is far worse, all mental, moral and spiritual diseases are contagious. An individual with a diseased viewpoint on life should be quarantined in the same way as a person with the smallpox. The germs that radiate from diseased lives are far more virulent that any ever discovered by science.

The student of alchemical philosophy must needs be an individualist. In modern medicine, physicians do not treat ailments; they treat individuals. Individualization is a property peculiar to all mental development and has consequently divided all human beings from one another, frequently also from the plan of Nature. In studying the animal we may study a species, but in studying man we must consider the individual to represent a unique type in every case. The problem confronting the student of human nature consequently is an ever-changing one, with as many angles as there are human minds. The power of choice that the mind exercises independently of Nature and whereby it elects to disobey Nature is the cause of nearly all the sorrow in the world today. All human beings have two natures; their truly human nature and their animal nature. The first is natural to man, while the second is natural to the beast. In crisscrossing, or changing, therefore, we have the false process of assumption; for man can assume an animal nature but it is always degenerating for him to do so.

During the last hundred years there has been a great revival of the Ancient Wisdom. Incidentally, there has also been a revival of certain things which do not pertain to the subject at hand. Thousands of people have studied the ancient Masters, with profit more or less according to their own basic natures. Most have assumed a great deal and have grown very little. The soul of man grows like the plant. It unfolds under the light of reason and lifts its face to gaze straight and unafraid at the power that gave it being.

The great Masters are spiritual gardeners who take care of the human flowers. The Master may love the human flower and tend it with all care, but only God, Nature, and its own inherent life can make it grow. And oh, how slowly it grows! You may sit down and watch it for hours and see no change. But in due time and in its own season it blossoms forth in all its glory, loved and admired by all who pass that way. God is the head gardener, Nature the fertile field, and we the growing plants. Let us make certain that we are really growing half as much as we think we are.

Are we really building a beautiful character of our own or merely renting one from someone else? Are we borrowing virtues from others or building them within? Are we spending our time fighting our failures or cultivating our virtues? Are we praying to the gods for more wisdom or making better use of each day of what we already have? These are questions which everyone must honestly answer, but there are very few honest people and hence few responses. If the average occult student could be bought for what he is worth and sold for what he thinks he is worth, fortunes would be made overnight.

The thoughts of other people can never vicariously become a part of you. You may take your choice, however, from all the wisdom of the world and make it your own by mental toil. There must always be the adjustment between the fact as it is in its simplicity, and the application of that fact to your own life. You must live upon knowledge like the plant that takes the soil of the earth and builds therefrom its delicate organism. Most disciples believe all they hear, and swear by their instructors. A few wise ones weigh all things and cling unto that which is good (in the sense of being useful). Each person should chew his own intellectual food, or at least digest it if he wishes to live upon its essences. The ancient adepts unfailingly impressed upon their disciples the necessity of the individual digesting, assimilating, and applying the things he was taught.

When this wisdom really becomes a part of you, and not merely a registered impression, you will find that it will begin to mold the tangible nature into a likeness of itself. Mere observation will prove that the student does not digest and apply the knowledge that he secures. Most cult-joiners are crazy—some mildly, other violently. The eternal question is, Why? The answer is obvious: They have overtax their minds with abstractions; they have tried to force the expression of virtues which they did not possess; they have tried to burst suddenly into bloom without building their virtues slowly and carefully as the plant does its form. When people try to be something they are not, they generally get into trouble. The only legitimate or practical method is by gradual development and growth. Then the candidate for Hermetic honors becomes an alchemist, gradually transmuting his entire nature into the thing that he desires it to be.

To grow gradually in a balanced manner is the true secret of success in mysticism. The nature must grow as an entirety. To be virtuous in one respect and neglect all others is to be inconsistent; and to be inconsistent is to destroy one's self. There is no use trying to reach heaven on a monorail track, for that form of locomotion failed years ago. A well-rounded nature is far more to be desired than one outstanding virtue and a dozen besetting sins.

In occultism, too much stress cannot be placed upon the interrelation of these factors. The candidate may eat certain foods or sleep with his head toward the North Star when he is doing certain things. But to do anything disconnectedly is very unwise. To be virtuous in speech but careless in thought is rank inconsistency, and the penalty of inconsistency is insanity. Consistency is a cardinal requirement of all students and is of far greater help than any single over-worked line of virtue.

# PART VI

# THE ROMANCE OF THE SPIRIT
# AND THE SOUL

The spirit in man is the divine spark, birthless, deathless, and untreated, but containing the power of creating as part of its immortality. It is the donor of life—that part of the immortal God which has taken up its dwelling place in the fourfold tabernacle of its children. This ancient Tabernacle (as described in the early Scriptures and also by Josephus) is, in reality, the living temple of the human body, and all its parts and utensils have their symbolic counterparts in the various functions and anatomical principles of the human body.

In a rare manuscript now unobtainable we find the entire Holy Land depicted as a human body. When we continue this analogy, the spirit in man assumes a position like unto what the ancient Talmudic priests called "The-Lord-Blessed-Be-He." The ancients also referred to this power as the Causal Man—the Ruler of that universe of effects which He has delivered out of Himself. He is the composite Elohim, male and female, father and mother, who, dividing Himself from Himself, became the Yin and Yang of China and the Isvara and Avalokitesvara of the ancient Hindus.

He—the Logos—becomes the perfect lord of His creation, and, having disseminated Himself into the not-self, He ordains for these disseminated parts the great pilgrimage or day of wandering, at the end of which these heterogeneous elements will be led back to their unified Cause. The wanderings of these germs of immortality through the vale of maya the ancient Jews called "the years in the wilderness." The tribes of Israel (the divine Duodecimo, preserved to our rather prosaic times as the cut-up man in the almanac), under the direction of Moses, still carry on their uncompleted search for the Promised Land.

Spirit is that central cohesive power which binds organisms together—a subtle effluvium in which the evolving granules float like the planets in the Pranic emanations of the sun. Pythagoras and other ancient philosophers thought that bodies are exuded from the spirit in the same way that a crustacean exudes the substances which later harden to form its shell. This is the arcane significance of the ancient Hermetic adage, that the "marrow gives birth to the bone." This spiritual monad is the Atman who, contemplating the great unreality, gathered the molecules by His magnetism and, passing them through His auric bodies, sent them forth permeated with Himself to form His worlds. These worlds, therefore, are called in Scripture "the daughters of men." In the same chapter the spirits are called "the sons of God." These sons of God saw that the daughters of men were fair and came down into them.

Grouping themselves together, these daughters of men formed the material world. They are the virgins of Nature who are set aside from all the world to become the brides of Christ. They are (as we will discuss later) the stones from which are built the New Jerusalem which is to be wedded to the Son of Light, according to Revelation. These bodies, moreover, have a voice, called by us the soul and by the Greeks, Psyche. This soul is a material thing in one sense of the word in that it is born in a manger surrounded by animal appetites. Born a son of man, it can ascend to the dignity of a son of God. Of course, we do not refer to the soul as a physical entity in this case, but rather to its principle which is understanding.

One of the leaves of Hermes' sacred tree bears upon it the significant alchemical word distillatio. This means to extract through a chemical process, usually requiring evaporation. We know that our daily life is a course in cosmic schooling. In one sense of the word, a child distills education from its academic researches. In a similar fashion, consciousness distills the products of wisdom and understanding from the complexities of life. This distillation was called by the ancients the soul, or the "perfect voice of the bodies."

You may have read the allegory of the pearl of great price which the diver seeks under the sea. The pearl represents the soul, the diver is the spirit, the diving suit represents his bodies, and the water is the physical world. As the prodigal son was nobler and truer as the result of his wanderings, so man learns to be as great as his gods by alchemical distillations from his experiences.

The spirit is immortal; the bodies are mortal, but from them can be extracted an immortal essence—wisdom. Psyche is symbolized with butterfly wings, for like the butterfly, she passes through a state of metamorphosis. The bodies are ugly worms or caterpillars, crawling upon the earth in their unredeemed and unrefined state. But, like the Eastern saint who, entering upon his meditations, is reborn into reality by his asceticism, so this ugly crawling thing, blackened with the earth, enters into its trance condition of chrysalis to be reborn as a glorious, multi-winged creature capable of flying high above the surface of the earth where once it was bound by its worm-like attributes. Recognizing this marvelous transformation, the Greeks used the butterfly Psyche to represent the final redemption of the unregenerate man.

For similar reasons, the frog and the serpent were sacred among the ancients, for the tadpole finally comes forth upon the land and the snake sheds its skin in the same way that man sheds his bodies, coming forth each year in a brand-new garment. This sublime thought has been ably expressed in the poem, The Chambered Nautilus.

As the bodies must first be transmuted before they can become immortal, philosophers have long explained this process by the love stories of mythology. The romance of the spirit and the soul is the true mystic interpretation of the underlying principle concealed in nearly every love story of Scripture and myth. The soul may be called "the experience body" of man. It is actually the lower nature that will later be drawn up to union with the higher consciousness to complete the androgynous creation. The soul will some time be the functioning body of spirit who will make himself known unto all peoples and unto all nations through his dearly beloved Son, who bears witness of him before all worlds. This Son is the soul, ransomed out of all iniquity, conceived of the Holy Ghost, and born of an immaculate conception. This is the Redeemer—Christos, "the fire oil," the transmuted essences of all bodies, the conservation of all forces, the proper usage of all natural energies. This universal energy, if it be dignified or lifted up, shall draw all men unto it; for when the brazen serpent is raised all who look upon it shall live. Experience is the fruit of the Tree of Life, and when man can eat thereof he shall know good and evil and shall be in truth as great as the gods.

The romance between the spiritual and the material my be understood by taking an example familiar to all Bible readers. The City of Jerusalem, adorned as a bride, is married to the Lamb, according to the allegories of the Book of Revelation. Jerusalem is built upon four hills, from which fact is derived its name, which means "a city of stacks." This is sometimes erroneously interpreted "the city of peace." The four hills are, Qabbalistically, the four beasts of Ezekiel, the four apostle-historians, and the four aspects of the Egyptian sphinx. They are also the four heads of Brahma. Naturally, they are the four bodies of man, which together form the substances from which the soul must be extracted by distillation. Each of us is a walled city, made up of billions of parts, each alive, each subservient to our will but each demanding justice, integrity, and kindliness from its ruler.

The body of the average person is metaphysically a prison, which eternally limits him and makes difficult the accomplishment of his dreams. He would tell the beautiful thoughts that come into his mind, but his tongue cannot describe them; he would reproduce the music that he hears in his dreams, but his fingers are too clumsy. So it goes, until at last many despair of ever bearing witness physically to the indwelling spirit. The wise, however, never despair, but by their daily labor and prayers bring closer the day of their liberation when they shall be transfigured by that glory which, though always within, cannot shine out through the darkened glass of untutored souls.

At last his body—the city of his soul—purified and glorified, dons its wedding garment and becomes the bride of that spirit which has long dwelt unrecognized and unrevered in its midst. This regenerated body is the robe of the high priest, "the garments of glory unto the Lord." It is the golden wedding garment of St. Paul without which the disciple cannot come to the wedding feast of the Lamb.

This is also a key to the Song of Solomon the king, probably the least understood and therefore the most reviled of all Scriptural writings of the Jewish and Christian world. What minister dares to read its chapters from his pulpit? Yet from all accounts it is as highly inspired as any other part of the Scriptures. For ages none have studied it, yet it contains some of the greatest lessons to be found in any Scripture of the world. The dark-skinned maiden of Jerusalem is the earth, and (by cosmic analogy) the planet and also the physical body of all nature; while

Solomon, as Masons have discovered, is a personification of the sun, the white-faced one whose power and kingdom no living king shall ever equal.

Here we come to another important problem. The story of Solomon and his wives has long been a cause of dissension among Christian advocates of monogamy. The name Solomon is derived from three words, SOL-OM-ON. The name conceals the trinity known as the three suns, and is also the name of the superior God in three different languages. We know that a solar system consists of a radiant center around which revolve a number of negative receptive bodies. As substance is the bride of spirit—for the negative is the servant of the positive—so the planets revolving in their orbits about the sun and all the created things of the universe were referred to by the Jews as the brides, wives, or concubines of the central Light.

Among the ancients the spirit was always considered masculine and substance feminine. This further explains the reason for using the foregoing symbols. These planets receive the light of the sun, are bathed in its glory, and exist only because of its beneficent powers. They are therefore called the brides of Solomon upon whom he showers his treasures. The sun, radiating its light upon the planets, adorns them with their flora and fauna; so it is said of the great king, "He robed his maidens in precious stones, jewels, and costly raiment." The materialist reads only the words and is offended, for he is of the earth; while the idealist sees the spirit and is glorified thereby. We must learn that there is great difference between the spirit of truth and the literal letter of the law.

In ancient days, those who served the altars of the temple were chosen from among the daughters of the earth. They came from the highest and noblest of families. While still children they were consecrated to the service of the sanctuary and were called

Vestal Virgins, for they served the altars of Vesta, the goddess of the earth, the home, and the family. In the ancient rituals these virgins were married to the gods, with fitting and imposing ceremonials. The same rite has been carried over into Christianity, where certain persons desiring to renounce the world take holy orders and become brides of Christ. Underlying this allegory is a deep and important meaning, for it conceals that spiritual nuptial—the Hermetic marriage—in which the lower nature promises to love, honor, and obey its own spirit.

As far back as mythology goes, we have the stories of the virgins of the earth. They have come down to us under the composite symbol of the Madonna. The child of the Madonna represents the perfect being—the Illuminated One born out of Nature, the Eternal Widow. He is that One that shall attain to God and things of the spirit, while Himself molded in the pattern of the earth. This Redeemer is the Christ-ened man, of whom the prophets have written. He, the product of Nature, has by distillation attenuated and rarefied his bodies so that they reflect the radiant light of the indwelling God.

Out of the laboratory of life, where seething chemicals portray the tortures of the agonized souls of Dante's hell, come those great sages and saviors who have led humanity along the pathway to omnipotence. They are the children of the Immaculate conception. They were the Widow's Sons, the children of the Fish, whose father deserted them and left the fish floating in the sea of eternity, but who were ordained by their father to redeem the world. They are all Joshuas, sons of Nun (fish), ordained to lead the children of Israel through the desert and into the Promised Land. A great soul rising out of the world to save it, because that soul loves the world, is portrayed as the man-child in the arms of the Madonna. Such a soul represents life coming forth out of form, spirit triumphing over matter, divinity rising out of Nature; for all things must be accomplished in Nature.

Among the Mohammedans, or more properly the children of Islam, it has been taught that a woman had no soul. It was believed that only through her husband would she ever be able to reach heaven. This belief has long held Islamic womanhood in bondage to an erroneous understanding of a great spiritual law. Our previous discussion of this subject should show what the Prophet really meant. The woman referred to by Mohammed was not a physical person but the negative principle of Nature, the earth, material substance, or the clay bodies. Incapable of self-redemption, the lower substances must be redeemed by the Spirit, the universal Savior, who died for the sin of the world. The raising of the dead is well symbolized in the story of the grip of the lion's paw in Masonry or in the raising of Lazarus in the early Christian mysteries.

The Islamites have taken a cosmic truth and applied it to individuals, resulting in a terrible mistake, but common, however, among religions which insist upon taking spiritual allegory for literal fact. If this attitude of literalism is insisted upon, Scripture must speedily lose its savor, for no one can possibly accept the literal stories who has passed through a modern high school. The blame should not be placed upon Scripture but upon the narrowness of scriptural translations and the lack of idealism in the human mind.

Body is incapable of self-salvation; it must be regenerated and transmuted as the result of intelligent direction from spirit. When it receives these divine impulses, it exchanges its sordidness for a greater and more glorious body, rising, Phoenix-like, from the ashes of its own morality.

In symbolism, all energies, vitalities, and spiritual powers are represented by the Father. All substances and elements in the visible universe are included under the great Mother. When this symbolism is understood, the Scriptures of nearly all people quickly reveal their cosmic import and explain their mysteries to the honest and sincere seeker.

Many times the question has been debated whether Biblical characters ever lived. Many assert Scripture to be entirely mythological, while others affirm it to be wholly historical. However, both these viewpoints drop out of sight as comparatively unimportant beside the all-dominating question, "What does Scripture mean to me now? How will it assist me to live better, to think better, to fill my place in the great plan of every-day existence?" The ancient occult records tell us that Jesus lived, but that his life (like all other lives, especially that riper kind long mellowed by experience) also bore witness to the plan of Nature.

The repentant Mary of Magdala washing the feet of her Lord and wiping them with her hair is of no value merely as an historical incident, but means a great deal when we see its hidden symbolism. Mary—the body—long servant of Rome, robed in the garments of Caesar, represents man functioning thoughtlessly in the animal world, wakening from its lethargy, the body turns to serve the spirit of love, humility, and beauty—the divine thing within itself. The woman in scarlet assumes the robe of white; the lower animal nature (the Red Sea) is crossed and, becoming the sole master of its own emotions, serves at last a nobler cause.

Again, the gentle Christ here depicted ceases to be an historical individual but sinks into his cosmic role as part of the cosmic allegory. The Christ spoken of is the Christ in you, the hope of glory, about which the Psalmist loved to sing. Personalities play parts in these dramas, but not important parts. In the physical world the masculine line is domineering, forceful, and offensive, usually demonstrating few of the finer qualities but dealing in weighty matters and clashing shields with the problems of material existence. He is the breadwinner usually, but must sacrifice the finer sensibilities, the intuitive powers, the love of beauty, art, and mysticism for the needs of every day life—that is, unless an abnormality occurs.

These finer instincts are the birthright of the feminine, for they represent soul qualities. Man was not created with the power of conceiving charity, kindness, or love. These he built into himself through the ages, as the distillation of experience. He had to earn the right to know beauty, and he earned it by suffering long for its lack.

Therefore, the eternal will of the Father is combined with that wisdom which is the fruitage of experience, and the one in whom these two are blended stands forth as a Savior of men. The two great opposites of Nature—father and mother principles—have been united in him. Therefore, he is said to be a son of the Hermetic marriage. He is his own father and his own mother, a priest after the order of Melchizedek.

# PART VII

# THE IMMACULATE CONCEPTION

It has often been said that one of the greatest problems of our civilization is that of the establishment of homes. The strength of a nation depends upon its homes. The moral character of a people is largely the result of the kind of training received during the first fifteen years of life. We have heard it said that those best fitted to marry do not, while those least fitted, people the world with organisms of such inferior quality that only the lowest forms of egos incarnate. This was presented to the ancient world under the mystery of the immaculate conception.

The idea of the immaculate conception is by no means original with Christianity. It is one of the oldest concepts of the human mind, for the gods of a hundred races and a thousand generations have been born of immaculate conceptions. In some mysterious way, then, even the half-sleeping mind of man seemed to realize that the world was ruled by an immutable law of cause and effect, and that a great and undefiled spirit could come into the world and manifest only through an undefiled body. So, when the gods found it necessary to take upon themselves bodies of clay and enter this world of defilement, these forms were prepared (so the Scriptures have told us) in a mysterious way. Their coming was heralded by hosts of angelic or spiritual beings called Devas. The mass of the human race felt that with the coming of a great mind something divine came into the world;

43

that its coming must be prepared for and its temple made as perfect as a man was capable of designing it.

Man is limited by his body, as we have said before, and body is limited by the things of which it is made, the conditions under which it came into the world, and the environments which surround it during the formative periods of life. The wise of all ages have known this. They knew that the better the body in organic quality, the broader the mind, the deeper the understanding, the more noble the position that such a one could reach in this world. Hence, they are said to have prepared in the temples the bodies for their saints and saviors, purifying the lives of the parents so that the coming creature might be free from those taints which normally are the birthright of man.

The Essenes, or Nazarites as they were called, were a group of holy men and women who lived in seclusion among the hills of the Holy Land and in a lamasery on the side of Mount Tabor. They are supposed to have been of Hindu origin, for they were ascetics in every sense of the word, spending much of their time in fasting and meditation. Legend relates that it was in their house that Joseph and Mary were trained and Jesus was educated prior to his ministry.

The great need of the world today is better bodies. Better bodies mean better lives and nobler outlooks. They mean more high-minded citizens, better able to meet the problems of life. Crime is largely the result of physical bodies that torment the souls of those trying to function through them. The viewpoint on life consequently becomes diseased, and lives of sorrow follow.

Out of the infinite, the law of attraction draws into incarnation lives and intelligences in harmony with the bodies in which they are to dwell. Our world is filled with suffering and sorrow because the bodies prepared for the birth of the race are so polluted and so carelessly considered that true and noble ideals cannot manifest through them. Great souls cannot enter. The immaculate conception must first become a reality in the world before the demigods of old can walk the earth again, for these great minds must have their vehicles built according to the law; and today the builders of bodies are lawless, thoughtless, irresponsible, and selfish to the nth degree.

Into the world come the things which they have thus drawn to themselves by virtue of the law of attraction. In response to this law, souls come to inhabit the bodies that they have built. Their parents pay the price by the incorrigibility of the lives which they have thereby evoked. There is but one answer: build better bodies. When this is done, a nobler and better race will come to dwell in them. This is the stupendous problem that humanity faces; and unless it be solved, race suicide is inevitable, for those who are coming in today are as unfit to give orders as they are unwilling to receive them.

Each ego coming into the world fashions its body not only according to the knowledge that it has gained in its evolution, but also according to the material at hand. In the case of the average infant, about all the little life has to labor with is ten generations of scrofula, and physical atoms of such low organic quality that the body can only be partly efficient at best. Diseased and hampered, broken even before birth, the ego has but two paths before it—the one, to come through and struggle on in a mediocre existence; the other, to remain waiting, hoping that some day a nobler vehicle will be prepared for it.

This is the way in which a race must gain its bodies, and is one of the reasons why the mighty civilizations of the past were overthrown by barbarians. The savage races (whose morality is much higher and life far more natural than ours), being free from the moral degeneracy of civilization, build better bodies and minds, and soon overwhelm those decadent races that have lost the power to give man his suitable birthright.

Behind the veil of maya great minds are waiting, waiting for an opportunity to come into the world in a way that will permit them to be efficient workers here and carry on the labor of building the ethical, moral, philosophical, and scientific structure of our civilization. Saints and sages are waiting, but there is no suitable place to which they may come, no homes where they can secure the spiritual, intellectual, and physical environment necessary for the manifestation of their highly evolved individualities. As a result, we have only a few great minds, but seething masses who are virtually useless and not a few who are criminal. These souls come, drawn by the law of attraction, because the environments are suitable for the development of their varying types of degeneracy.

Behind the veil dividing the living from the dead are the answers to the riddles of science and the mysteries of all ages. But great souls cannot come or be known here until the bridge is built between the living and the unborn; until ideal homes are found and efficient bodies are built in which they may function true to the great law of progress.

With fear and trembling we face the future of the race, which is doomed to disaster unless the immaculate conception becomes a reality. The immaculate conception is not a miracle. It is realization of the responsibilities of parenthood, in which by right living, right thought, and right attitude an opportunity is given for higher and nobler souls to incarnate and glorify the world by their presence. This is the story of the birth of Jesus, who, watched over by the priests, was given a body as nearly perfect as the conditions of that age would permit.

This same miracle can be repeated whenever man will live to serve his fellow men, thereby giving the highest and best within himself an opportunity to manifest itself. The future of the race rests in the hands of its mothers and fathers—in these children coming into the world today, many of them uncurbed and undisciplined. Through thoughtlessness and criminal negligence, parents are dooming their race to destruction by sending its lawmakers of tomorrow on their way through life unenlightened, uninformed, and unprepared.

The Master told the story in the parable of the new wine in old bottles. He recognized the fundamental need of a new organization for a new idea, the fundamental need of a new, clean body as the major factor in growth and progress. If we do not prepare higher types of bodies for those higher grades of intelligence necessary to rule a civilization, then a new race will have to be given to the world that the spirit of progress may not be thwarted.

Heredity is not a spiritual heritage, for a man inherits only from himself in the spiritual sense of the word. It does hold true to some degree, however, with regard to the substances from which bodies are made. The immaculate conception is therefore a vital factor in heredity, for it teaches that to noble parents come noble children, while those whose attitudes and ideals are false can give to the world only plagues that are worse that nothing at all. Spiritual heredity draws lives into incarnation through type attraction; physical heredity limits the body in its efficiency to the material from which it is formed.

As a philosophical problem, the immaculate conception may be summarized as follows; Immaculate means clean; it has nothing to do with miracles. The immaculate conception means a clean birth, in which the highest and finest of Nature's laws are brought to bear upon the masterpiece of Nature's labors—the formation of bodies for the habitation of living beings.

# PART VIII
## SUMMARY

In conclusion, we may consider three problems: celibacy, as applied to occult students; the Hermetic marriage, as an alchemical process; and the mystery of individual completeness.

All advanced candidates on the path of occultism, mysticism, and kindred subjects must take the oath of celibacy for two very good reasons: (1) They are unfitted for connubial life. Havelock Ellis has said that among the ministry are found not only some of the brightest children in the world but also more imbeciles that in any other profession. The advanced specialist in occult work is carrying on his spiritual investigations with the transmuted essences of those forces which are normally used in reproduction. (2) Because the candle cannot be burned at both ends, marriage for such types is unfair to all parties concerned. It is often fatal to the occultist, for at a certain time the barriers which separate the brain from the generative system are removed, and insanity or death will follow those who are not as fully in control of their emotions as their position demands.

All the world, however, is not made up of adepts or great initiates. Consequently, the assumption of the state of celibacy by people who have no idea of the meaning of such an act has caused much sorrow and suffering. The occultist must remember that nature is consistent. Celibacy is one of many things which make an adept. However, he does not become an adept through one thing alone: his entire life must be harmonized, and celibacy is merely one of many means which together produce the desired end.

Modern occultism has too many fads; dieting, fasting, meditating, and a host of other things are held out as methods of obtaining spiritual powers. The jewel of all, however, is consistency. To break all the written and unwritten laws and play on a one-stringed instrument of virtue is foolish and unbalanced. All things must work together. He must eat in harmony with his thoughts, meditate in harmony with his actions, pray in harmony with his daily life. Being in harmony, he is great; and being consistent, he is wise.

It is useless to develop spiritually at any single point or to try to assume a virtue which is not part of the nature. Instead of being exceptionally virtuous concerning what you eat and completely vice-ridden in everything else, try being normally careful in all things. Spiritualize the animal nature gradually; do not seek to make a god out of a fool over night. A great occultist was once asked, "What are the stages of human growth?" He said, "To the animal man, indulgence in all things; to the human man, moderation in all things; to the divine man, abstinence in all things earthly."

Friends, please do not forget these most important words, "in all things." The fanatic overdoes some one thing; therefore he becomes unnatural and insane. The wise man, however, grows gradually, overdoing nothing but building so symmetrically that he will not backslide within the first week.

While a person is striving to be good he has not yet attained virtue, for virtue lies in transmuting the desire to do that which is not right to the point where it naturally desires to do good.

Many people tell us how they have sacrificed everything for others, expecting us to be impressed. What use is the gift without the giver? People who give in the spirit of sacrifice have small credit coming to them, for only those truly give who do it for the love of it. In all the relationships of life, therefore, let spiritual growth be symmetrical. Do not be a fanatic, for fanatics and prudes alike are the deadly enemies of virtue. Build and grow in a healthy way. Do not forget to laugh; do not forget to cry; but build each day into the nature those enduring principles of equity, justice, and right, which will produce a consistent occultist.

The Hermetic marriage is an alchemical symbol found in the nature of all things, for the law of polarity is universal. In the human world it appears as sex—positive and negative, masculine and feminine. As all electricians know, positive and negative are opposite poles of one circuit. Spirit itself knows no polarity, but manifests through polarity to the accomplishment of the Great Work. Superiority or inferiority of sex, consequently, is a fallacy and hallucination. Being in himself androgynous, each individual has one of these natures dominant and the other receptive. Marriage, as a human relationship, is merely an institution whereby two persons make a contract per verba de future cum copula. Its actual purpose is twofold: (1) to fulfill the natural law of polarity in the reproduction of the species; (2) to fulfill the spiritual law of association whereby the latent side of each nature may be stimulated by association with the personified exemplification of its functions, qualities, and powers in the other. In simple language, years of association result in each sex assuming to a marked degree the viewpoints, attitudes, feelings, and individuality of the other. The masculine mind in association with the feminine heart, consciously or unconsciously, becomes more or less softened, thereby preventing too strenuous expression of the material intellect. On the other hand, the feminine emotionalism and artistic sense, by association with the practical masculine temperament, becomes more independent and individual, and is thereby prevented from becoming one-sided.

Please remember that we are trying to express the purpose for which the institution of marriage was established. The lack of cooperation in the world today has thwarted this purpose to a great degree. Selfishness and a score of other major and minor sins have entered into the domestic relationship until it has lost nearly all semblance to its former self. As a result, the human race has missed the opportunity to acquire balance and symmetry. Ignoring the actual meaning of life's relationships and deluded by the idea that happiness is to be found in irresponsibility, mankind has strayed far from the path fixed by Nature for its creatures.

In due time the androgynous man will reappear, balanced and perfected in all those things which he now lacks. This will not be a racial move, but in every instance an individual attainment. To this end the race is laboring at the present time; but the individual will never gain the end until he reflects upon the serious side of life and learns that he is in the world to secure his spiritual and moral education.

The dual-headed man of Michael Maier is symbolic of the double consciousness of man: reason as the masculine head and intuition as the feminine head. These two heads not only rule the individual, but they also rule the race as the statecraft and the priestcraft. The priest after the Order of Melchizedek, was termed "priest-king" to symbolize his dual office, which is also symbolically portrayed by the two cherubim on the mercy seat of the ark of the covenant and by the onyx stones on the shoulders of the high priest. The so-called modern institution of marriage is, in reality, the manifestation of the Trinity; for father, mother, and son are a part of the divine order. The child represents the soul of the parents, for to a great degree its life bears witness of its progenitors.

Individual completeness is the end of all individual effort. Perfect adjustment between the spirit of man and his bodies results in the re-establishment of the androgynous man. It is the end of the path of growth as far as we know. The symbol of this accomplishment is the philosopher's stone, the rose diamond of the Rosicrucians, and the great pearl of the Illuminati. All the things which we see are but means to an end: to be met, to be battled, and to be conquered, as Caesar might have said.

The Hermetic marriage is symbolic of the individual who has made himself right with all things, and (most of all) is true to himself and to his fellow men. Human relationships lead to divine relationships, and the unfolding soul builds ever more noble mansions as vehicles for its expression. Only through the broadened vista of philosophy does man see hope; for the narrow-minded, things are seemingly hopeless. If behind the apparent chaos the spirit can still discern the divine order which is moving him slowly but persistently towards adjustment with himself, he will then be able to recognize the myriad ways in which the desire of the Infinite is made known to His finite creations.

Out of the present maelstrom of perverted sexology the philosopher can see a more noble spirit arising—not one who in a lofty way has avoided the endless pitfalls, but one who, nauseated with falsity and sham, has risen to loftier aspirations. The great task of our age is to dignify human relationships; to return the divine crown to the head upon which it belongs; to purify, cleanse, and redeem all things; to transmute civilization as one would transmute a personal habit. The Hermetic Marriage is the apotheosis of the world's most abused institution, which will rise again from the slime into which it has sunk; for in its proper recognition and application we see the hope of the race.

## Works on Occult Philosophy by Manly P. Hall

### MAN, THE GRAND SYMBOL OF THE MYSTERIES:
#### Thoughts in Occult Anatomy

This unique volume of thought-provoking essays shows how the human body reveals the laws and principles operating throughout the universe. Illustrated with plates from rare works on Rosicrucianism, Hermetic sciences, cabala, and more traditional texts on anatomy and physiology. Comprehensive index.

**$12.00. Hardback. 254pp. ISBN: 0-89314-513-0**
**$8.00. Paperback. 254pp. ISBN: 0-89314-389-8**

## Pamphlets on Occultism by Manly P. Hall

### MAGIC, A Treatise on Esoteric Ethics

An essay enabling individuals to distinguish between "black" and "white" magic, thereby avoiding practices and disciplines which may be detrimental to character and dangerous to physical health.

**$5.95. Pamphlet. 72pp. ISBN: 0-89314-384-7**

### THE SACRED MAGIC OF THE QABBALAH: The Science of Divine Names

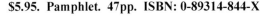

This essay sheds light on the doctrines of the old rabbis and the Pythagoreans regarding the science of the divine names and the mystery of numbers.

**$5.95. Pamphlet. 47pp. ISBN: 0-89314-844-X**

### UNSEEN FORCES

An illustrated treatise on the denizens of the invisible worlds, including the *"Dweller on the Threshold,"* and the individual's connection with them.

**$5.95. Pamphlet. 55pp. ISBN: 0-89314-385-5**

## Visit Our Online Catalog at www.prs.org

## ABOUT THE AUTHOR

Manly P. Hall founded the Philosophical Research Society, Inc., a non-profit organization in 1934, dedicated to the dissemination of useful knowledge in the fields of philosophy, comparative religion, and psychology. In his long career, spanning more than seventy years of dynamic public activity, Mr. Hall delivered over 8000 lectures in the United States and abroad, authored over 150 books and essays, and wrote countless magazine articles.

VISIT US AT WWW.PRS.ORG

ISBN: 0-89314-841-5

ISBN-10: 0-89314-841-5
ISBN-13: 978-0-89314-841-6